P9-DMB-801

Blue on Blue

Dianne White

Illustrated by Beth Krommes

Beach Lane Books • New York London Toronto Sydney New Delhi

MAR 0 5 2015

PROPERTY OF
SENECA COLLEGE
LIBRARIES
KING CAMPUS

Special acknowledgments to Kathi Appelt and my fellow Vermont College
Picture Book classmates: Mary, Randall, Joanie, and Wendy—D. W.

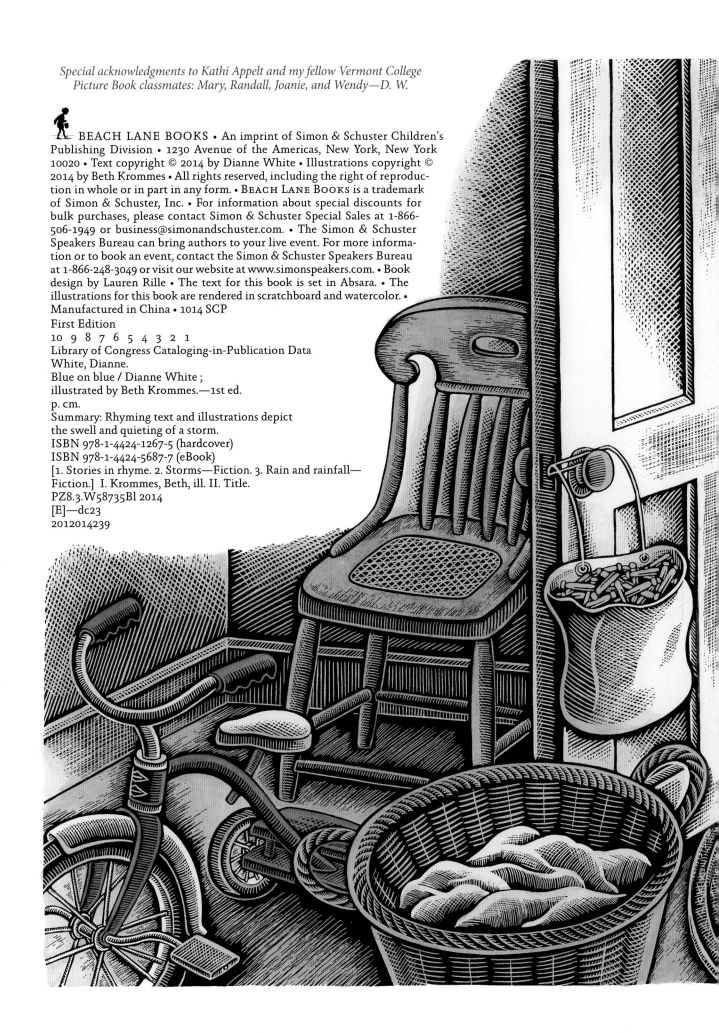

BEACH LANE BOOKS • An imprint of Simon & Schuster Children's
Publishing Division • 1230 Avenue of the Americas, New York, New York
10020 • Text copyright © 2014 by Dianne White • Illustrations copyright ©
2014 by Beth Krommes • All rights reserved, including the right of reproduc-
tion in whole or in part in any form. • BEACH LANE BOOKS is a trademark
of Simon & Schuster, Inc. • For information about special discounts for
bulk purchases, please contact Simon & Schuster Special Sales at 1-866-
506-1949 or business@simonandschuster.com. • The Simon & Schuster
Speakers Bureau can bring authors to your live event. For more information or to book an event, contact the Simon & Schuster Speakers Bureau
at 1-866-248-3049 or visit our website at www.simonspeakers.com. • Book
design by Lauren Rille • The text for this book is set in Absara. • The
illustrations for this book are rendered in scratchboard and watercolor. •
Manufactured in China • 1014 SCP
First Edition
10 9 8 7 6 5 4 3 2 1
Library of Congress Cataloging-in-Publication Data
White, Dianne.
Blue on blue / Dianne White ;
illustrated by Beth Krommes.—1st ed.
p. cm.
Summary: Rhyming text and illustrations depict
the swell and quieting of a storm.
ISBN 978-1-4424-1267-5 (hardcover)
ISBN 978-1-4424-5687-7 (eBook)
[1. Stories in rhyme. 2. Storms—Fiction. 3. Rain and rainfall—
Fiction.] I. Krommes, Beth, ill. II. Title.
PZ8.3.W58735Bl 2014
[E]—dc23
2012014239

For Robin,
who loves a good
rainstorm more than
anyone I know—D. W.

For my family,
with special thanks
to Marguerite—B. K.

Cotton clouds.
Morning light.

Blue on blue.
White on white.

Singing, swinging outdoor play.

White on blue on sunny day.

Clouds swell.
Winds blow bolder.

Weather changes.
Air grows colder.

Gray on gray. Dark and glooming.

Black on black. Storm is looming.

Thunder!
Lightning!
Raging, roaring.

Rain on rain on rain is pouring.

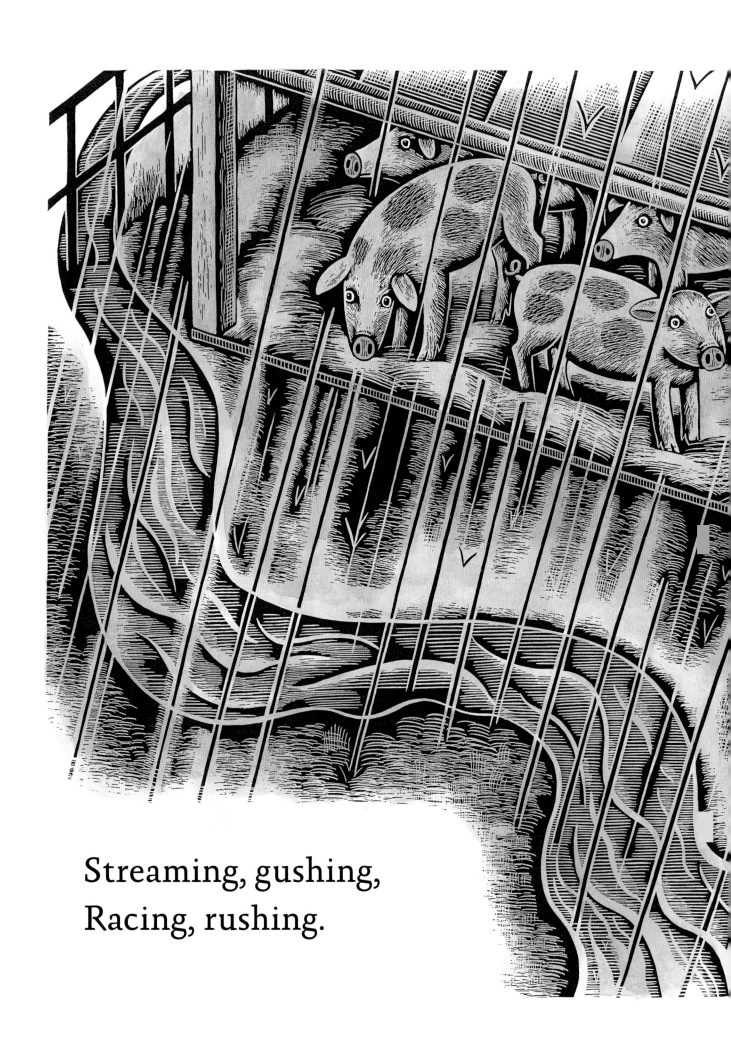

Streaming, gushing,
Racing, rushing.

Rain on rain on rain.

Pounding, hounding,
noisy-sounding.

Dripping, dropping. Never stopping.

Never stopping. Dripping, dropping.

Rain

on rain

on rain.

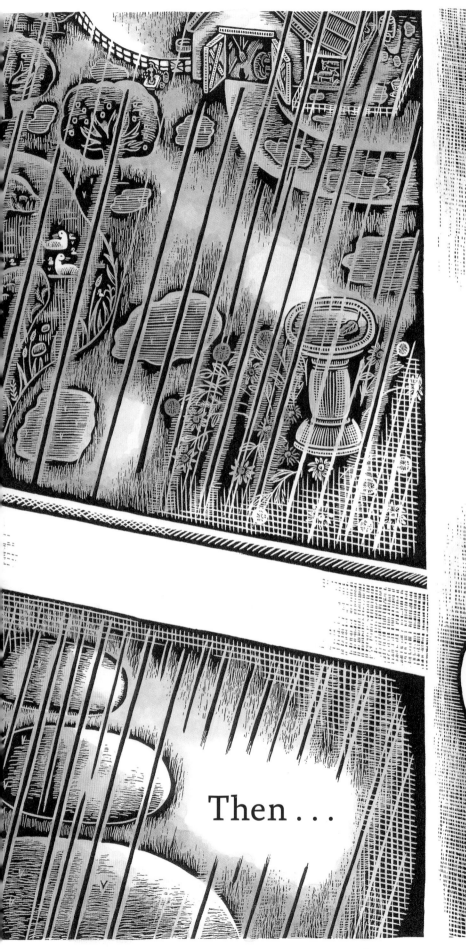

Then . . .

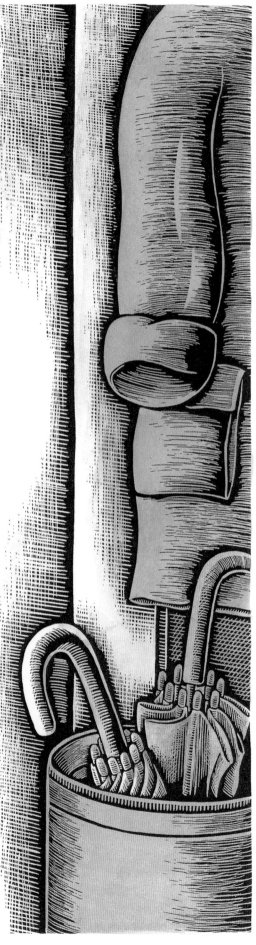

Winds shift.
Drops drip.

Drip, drop!
Drip, drop!

Slowly . . .
slowly . . .

slowly. . . .

Stop!

Sun sneaks back.
Warms the air.

Muddy, muddy . . .

everywhere!

Sun sets.

Time to go.

Moon rises.
Golden glow.

Glitter stars, twinkling light.

Black on gold . . .

on silver night.

PROPERTY OF
SENECA COLLEGE
LIBRARIES
KING CAMPUS